WELCOME TO ETERNIA

I am _____.

I am the defender of the secrets of Castle Grayskull.

Fabulous secret powers were revealed to me the day I held aloft
my magic sword and said, "By the Power of Grayskull! I have the power!"

I became the Master of the Universe!

Together, my friends and I defend Grayskull
from the evil forces of Skeletor!

BuzzPop

An imprint of Little Bee Books
New York, NY
MASTERS OF THE UNIVERSE™ and associated trademarks and trade dress
are owned by, and used under license from, Mattel. ©2021 Mattel.
Illustrated by Diego Vaisberg
All rights reserved, including the right of reproduction in whole or in part in any form.
BuzzPop and associated colophon are trademarks of Little Bee Books.
For information about special discounts on bulk purchases,
please contact Little Bee Books at sales@littlebeebooks.com.

Manufactured in China   RRD 0821
First Edition
10 9 8 7 6 5 4 3 2 1
ISBN 978-1-4998-1277-0

buzzpopbooks.com

By the Power of Grayskull!
I have the power!

Adam

You finally used that sword the way
it was meant to be used, Boy.

Skeletor

Cringer: How 'bout
we sit this one out 'til
the bad guys go away?

He-Man: Sitting's
for quitting.

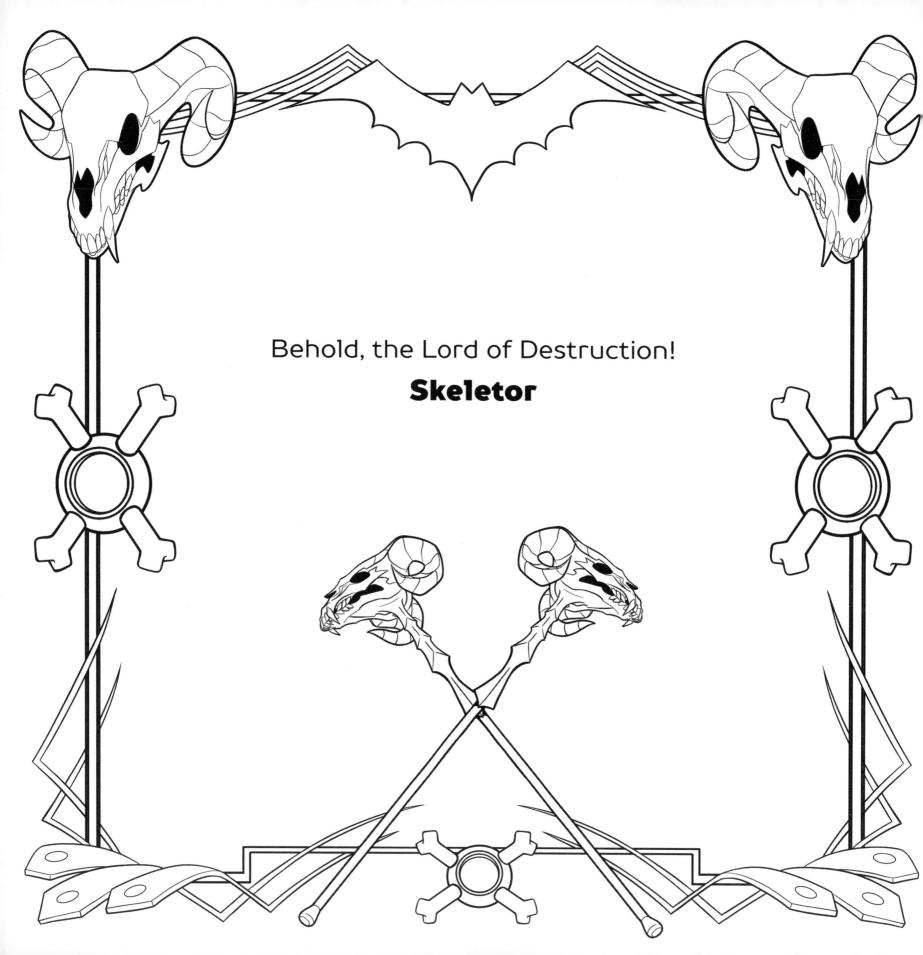

Behold, the Lord of Destruction!

Skeletor

I've come to tear Grayskull down,
stone by stone!

Skeletor

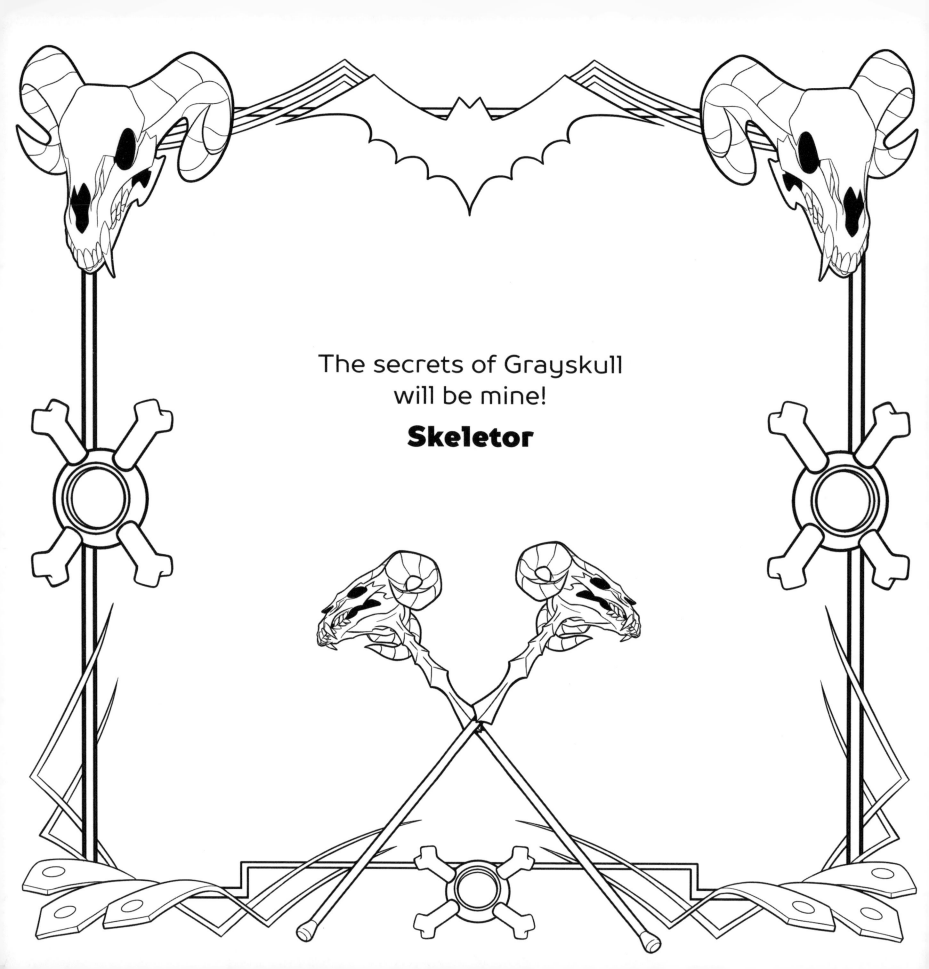

The secrets of Grayskull will be mine!

Skeletor

Evil-Lyn: You were always going on and on about He-Man.

Teela: You used to go on and on about Skeletor!

I'm your worst nightmare.

Teela

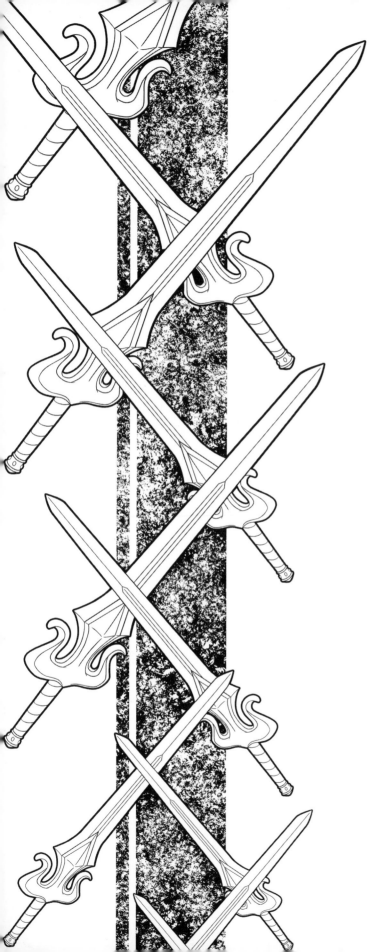

Teela: I've fought the forces of Snake Mountain. Did you think I couldn't defend against your attack?

Adam: That attack is called a *hug*, Teela.

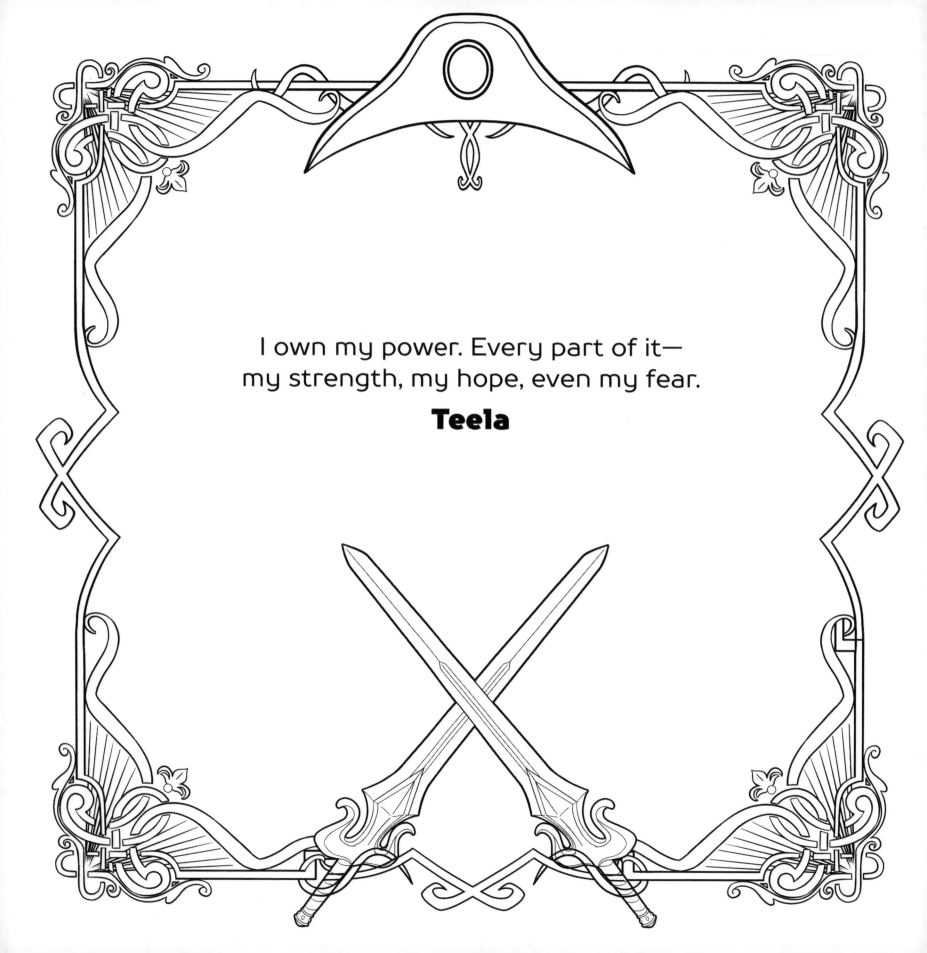

I own my power. Every part of it—
my strength, my hope, even my fear.

Teela

You're no match for the
malevolent magic of Evil-Lyn!

Skeletor

I'm not *clawful*,
but I can be awful!

Evil-Lyn

My devotion to Skeletor blinded
me to the obvious: that I could've
been a Master of the Universe.
I was born to rule! But instead
of fulfilling my destiny, I spent a
lifetime helping him fulfill his.

Evil-Lyn

I'm charging you with
a sacred mission.

Sorceress

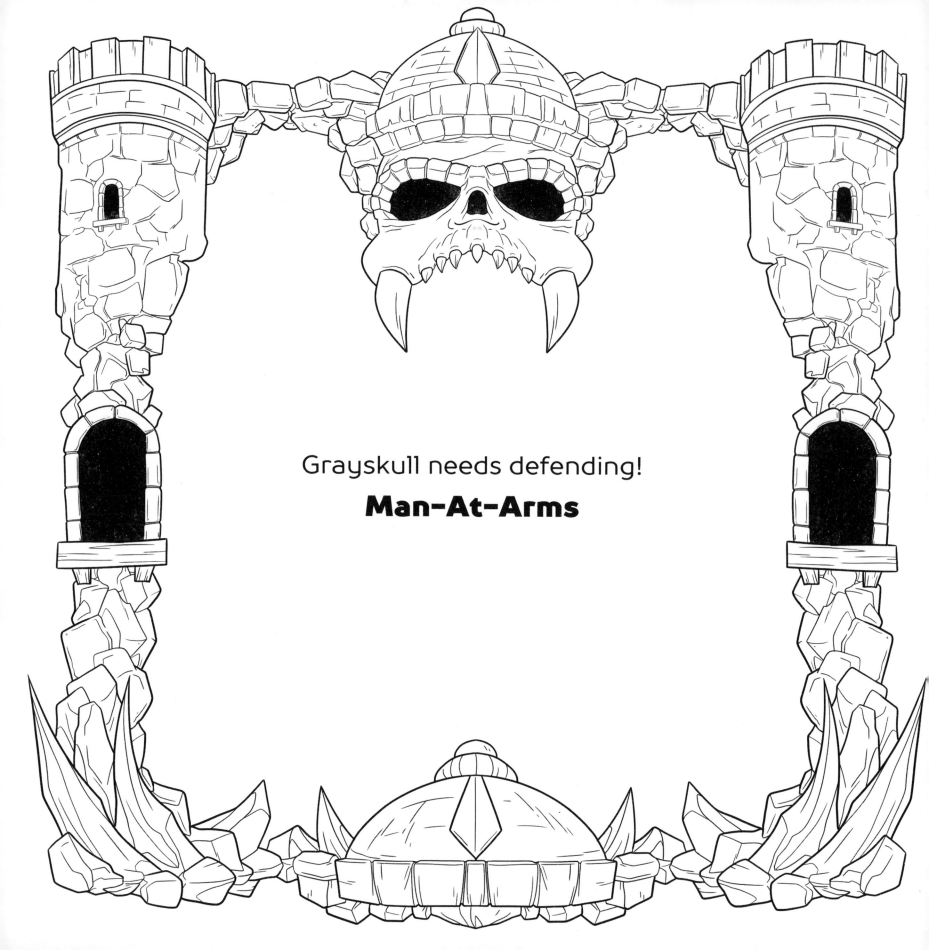

Grayskull needs defending!

Man-At-Arms

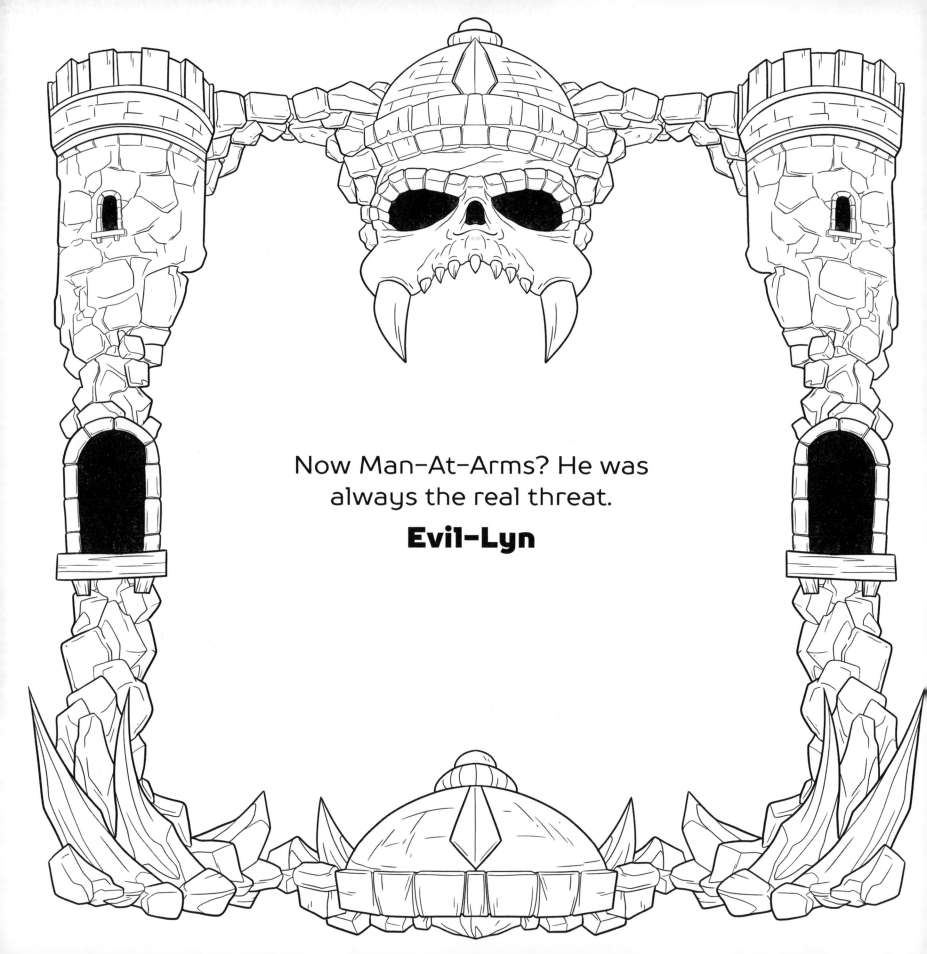

Now Man-At-Arms? He was always the real threat.

Evil-Lyn

Write down everything you ever do—
even the silly stuff you think is forgettable.
Because when the adventures are over,
that's all you're left with: good friends
and happy memories.

Orko

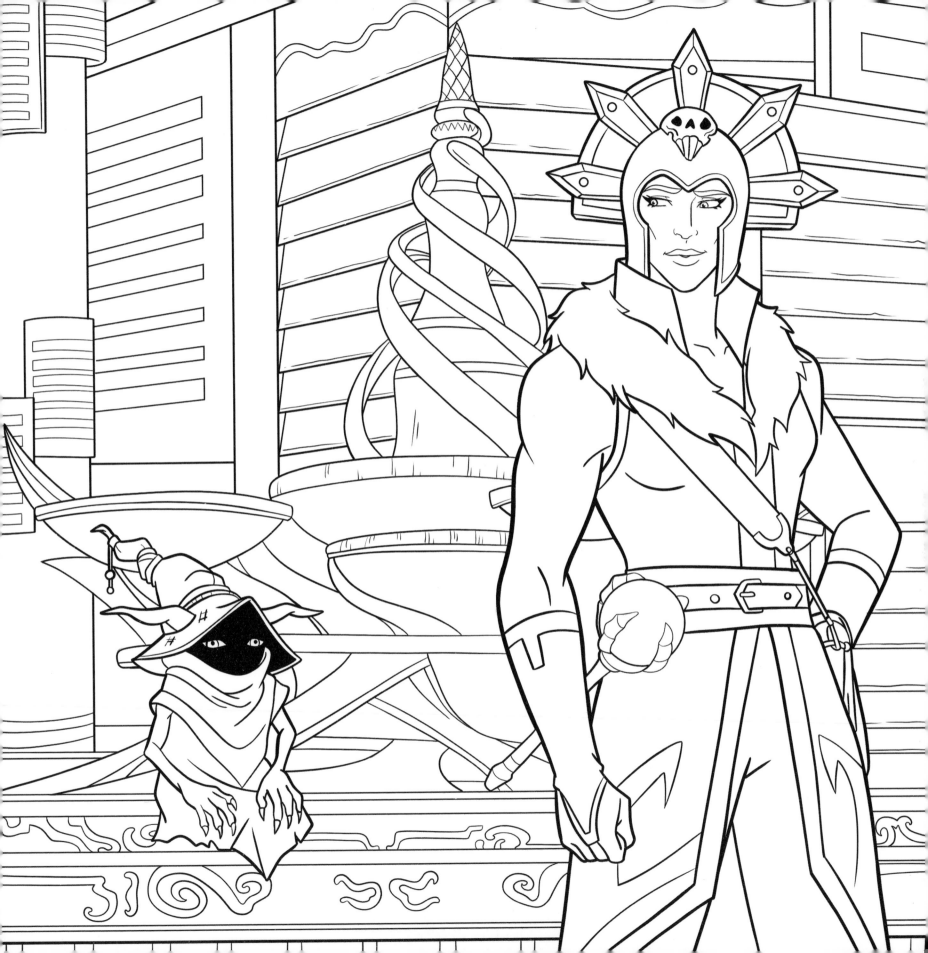

I don't need to walk.
I can float!

Orko

We don't have time for any more fighty-fighty!

Cringer

Don't let old bitterness
stand in the way of new hope.

Cringer

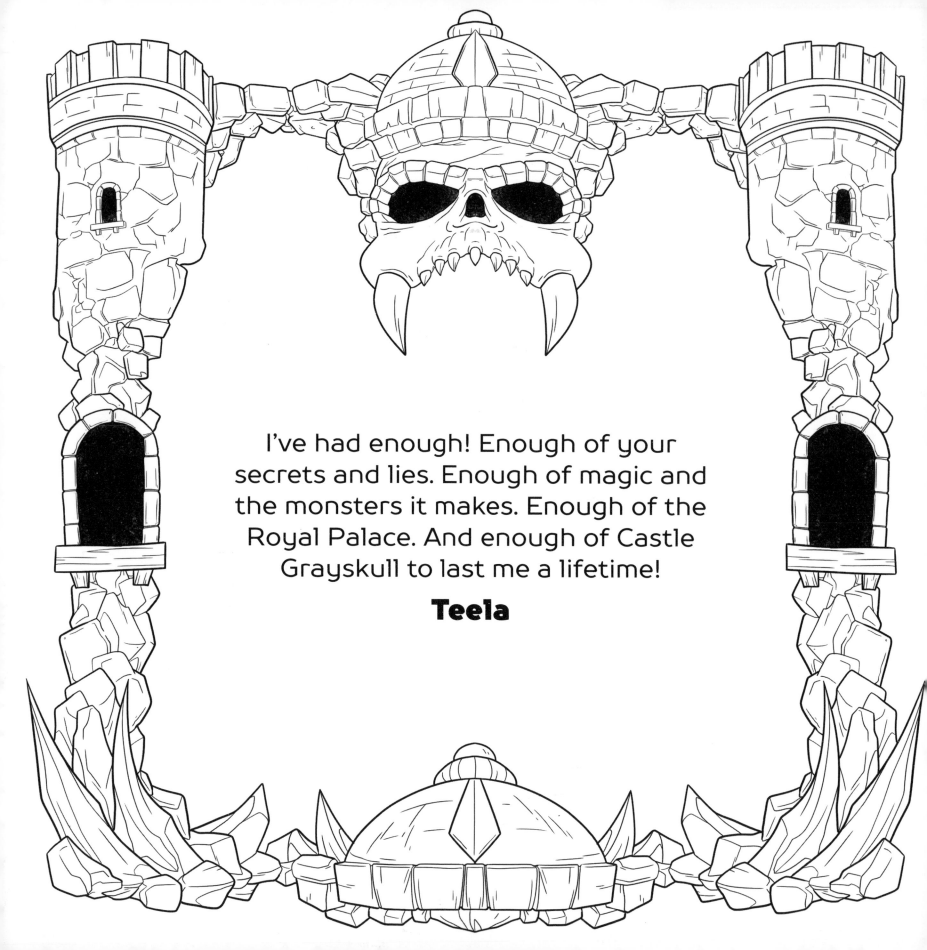

I've had enough! Enough of your secrets and lies. Enough of magic and the monsters it makes. Enough of the Royal Palace. And enough of Castle Grayskull to last me a lifetime!

Teela

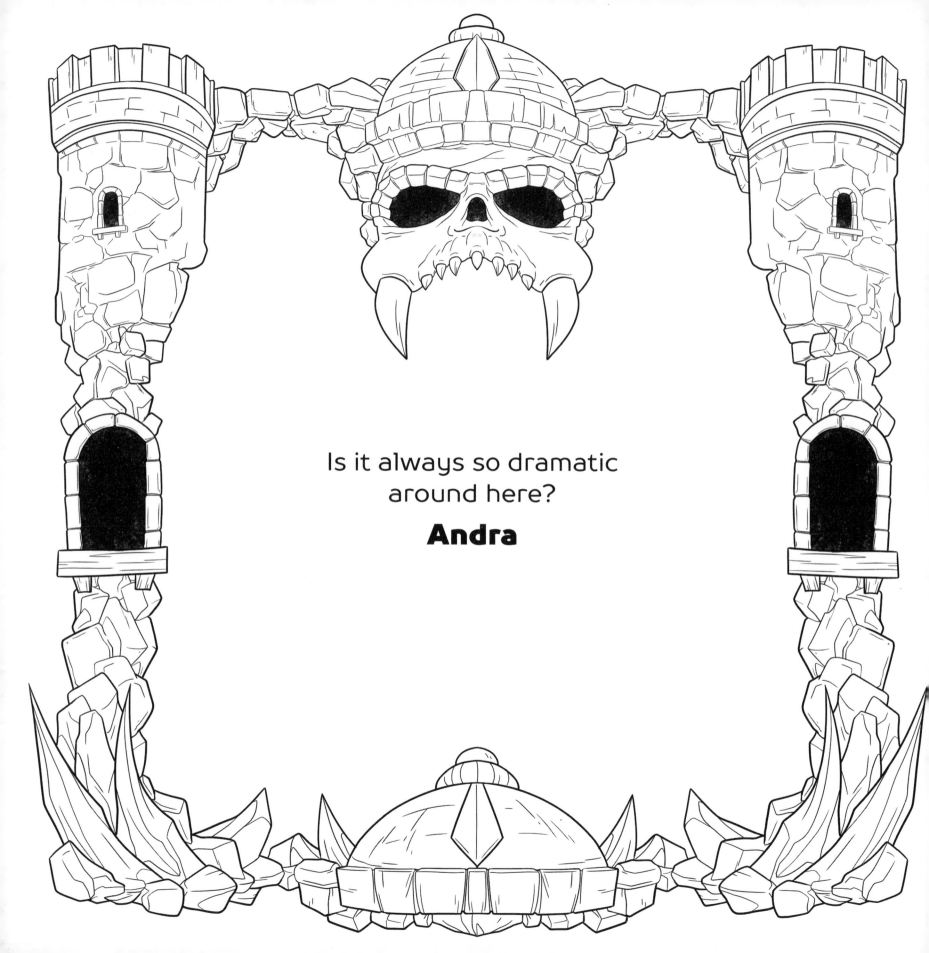

Is it always so dramatic
around here?

Andra

I'm the brains.
She's the brawn.

Andra

Did you really think your latest ruse
could fool the Sorceress of Grayskull?

Sorceress

You will never succeed, Skeletor.
Because you're not the Lord of Destruction.
You're nothing but the Lord of Failure.

Sorceress

Whether you serve Grayskull
or Snake Mountain, we all
gotta work together now.

Cringer

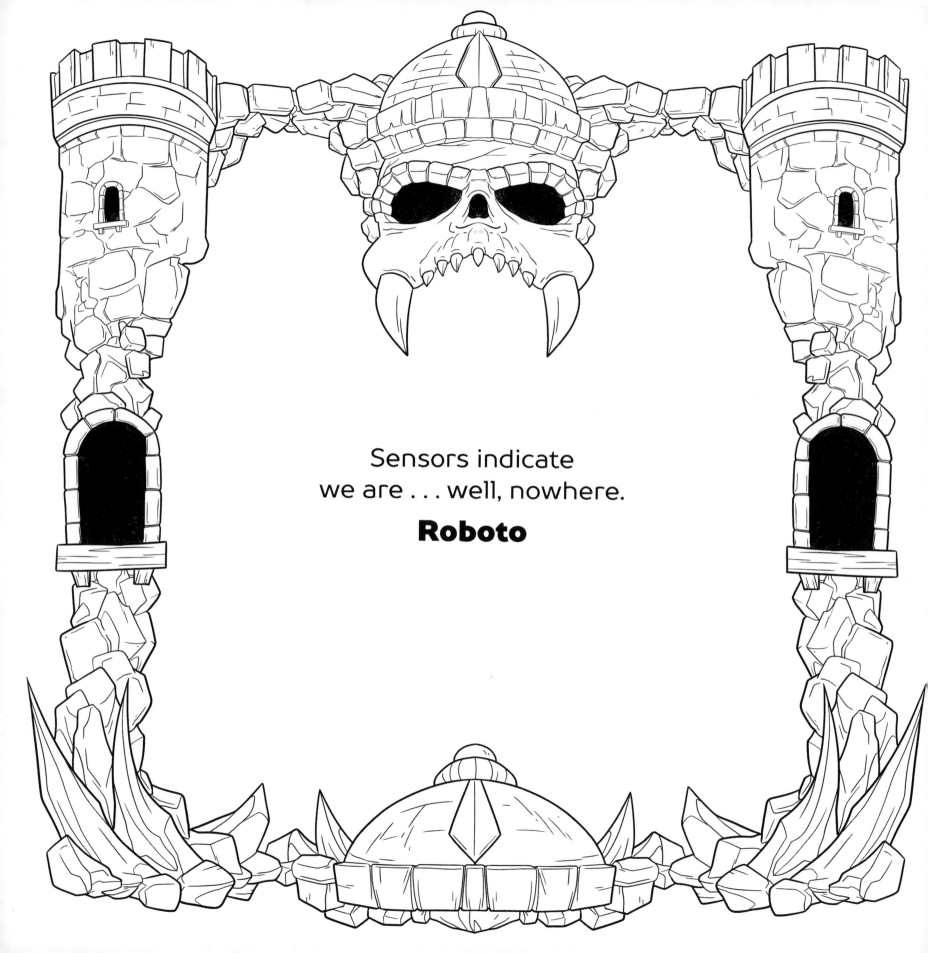

Sensors indicate
we are . . . well, nowhere.

Roboto

I operate from all of your memories.
Which means if you know how to reforge
the Sword of Power, then so do I.

Roboto

I try to keep things
Snake Mountain simple.

Beast Man

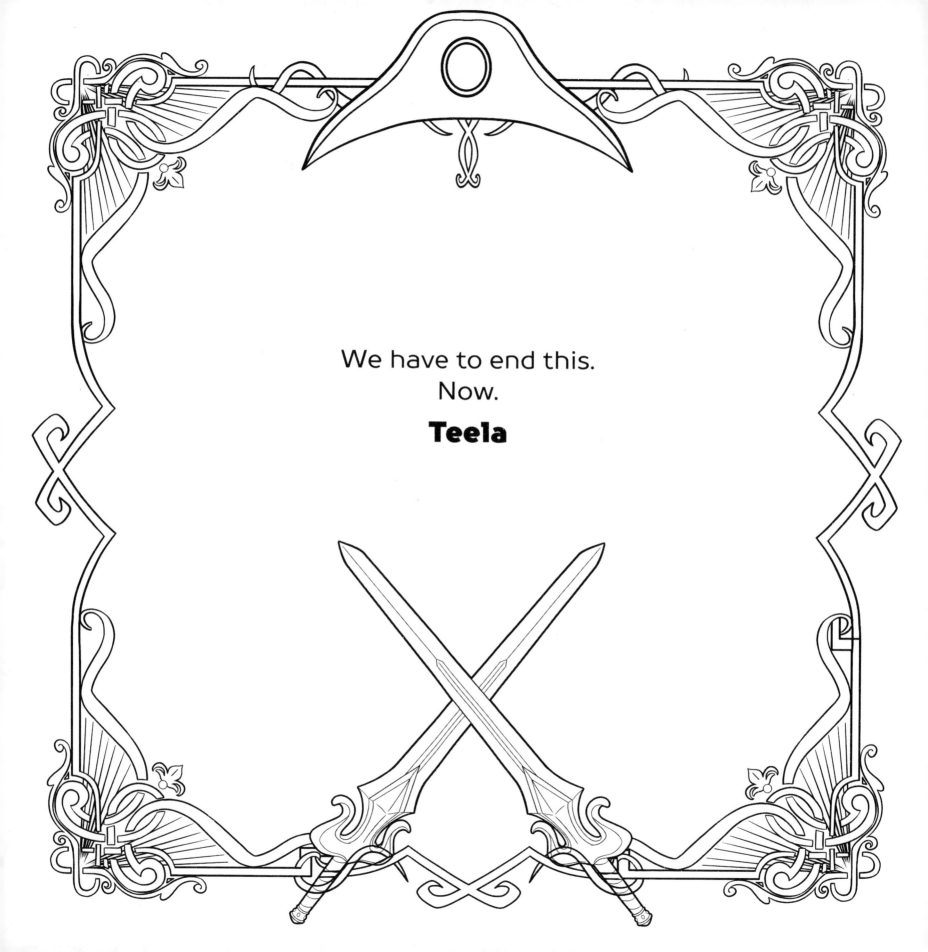

We have to end this.
Now.

Teela

You defile the heart of Grayskull
with your very presence!

Moss Man

As my dad says, "No amount of preparation can make you ready for the unpredictable."

Adam

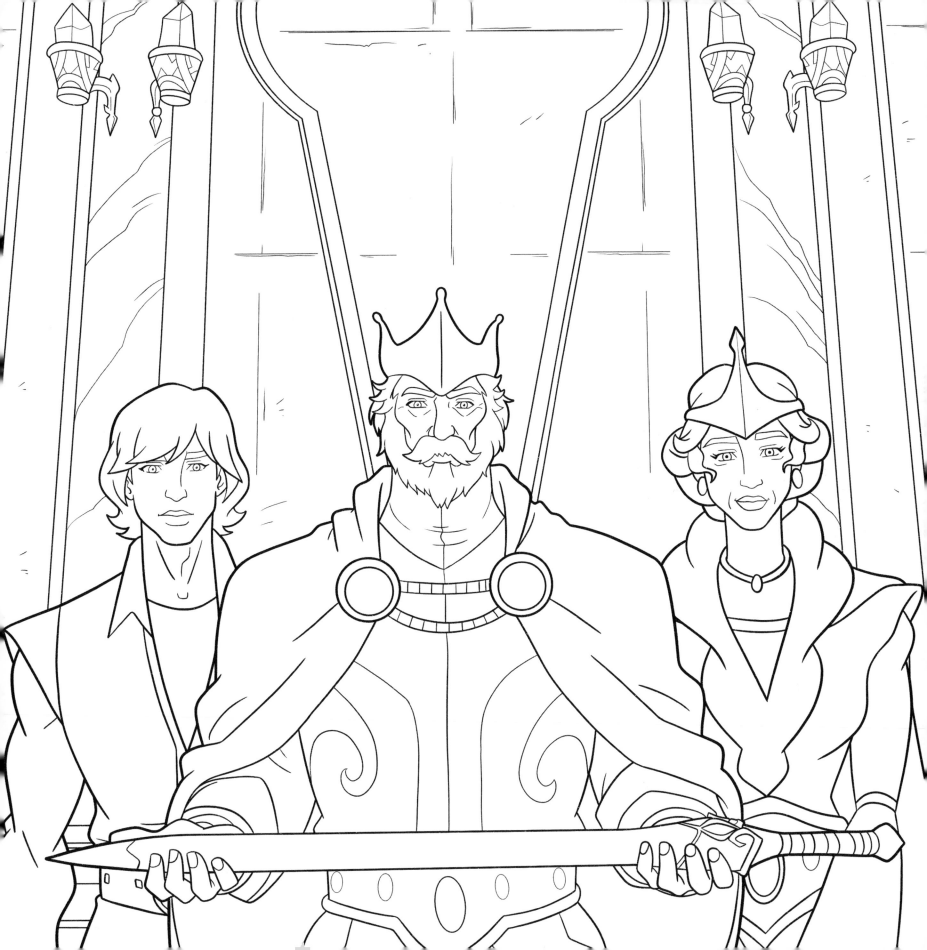

You must have
died a glorious death!

Grayskull

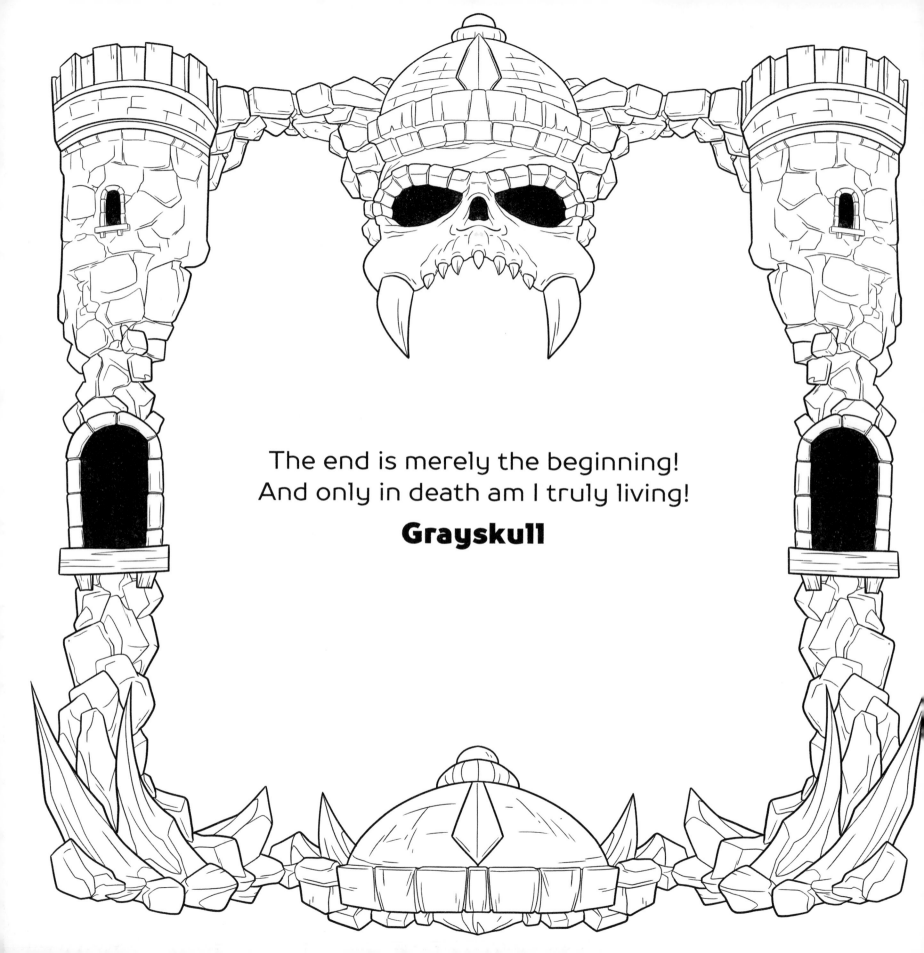

The end is merely the beginning!
And only in death am I truly living!

Grayskull

King Randor: It's said the great heroes live on for all time, in Preternia—

Queen Marlena: But, no one knows for certain.

Grayskull: Welcome to the winner's circle, Flea-man!

Wun-Dar: We call him that because he's small! Like a flea.

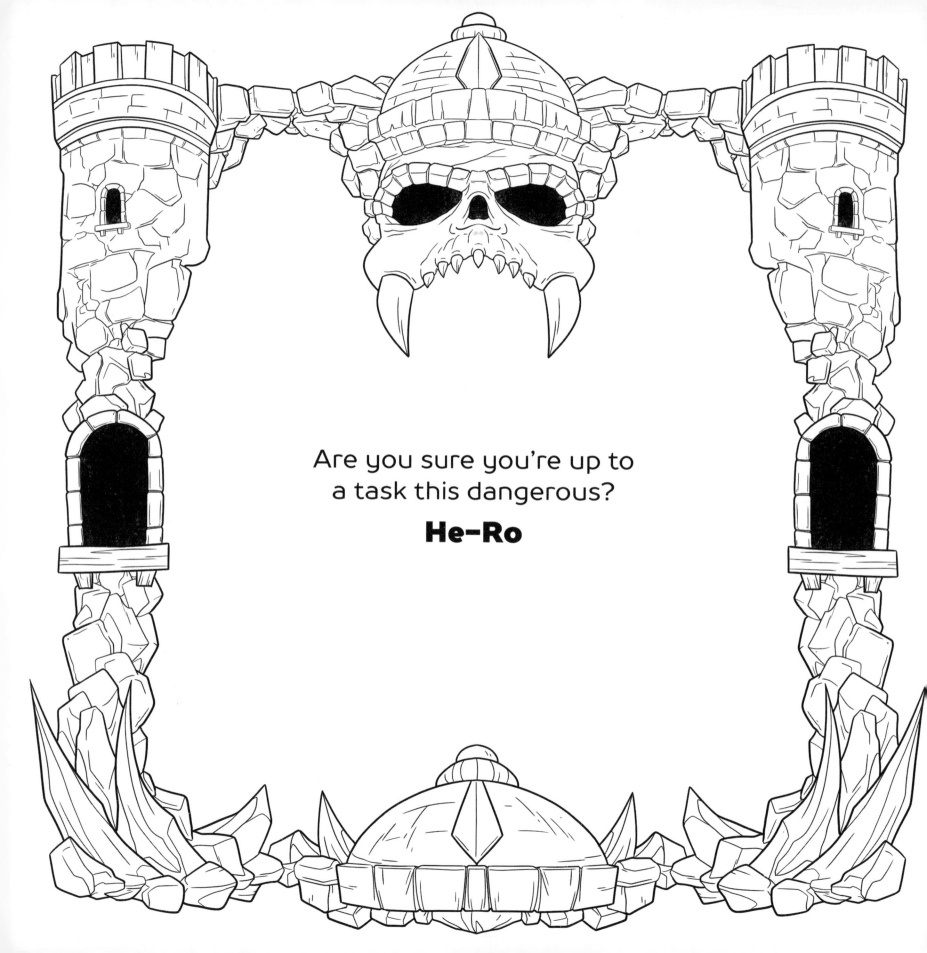

Are you sure you're up to
a task this dangerous?

He-Ro

Turns out,
nobody's born "evil."

Orko

Glory be unto we who live and *die-ode* in the mighty Motherboard!

Tri-Klops

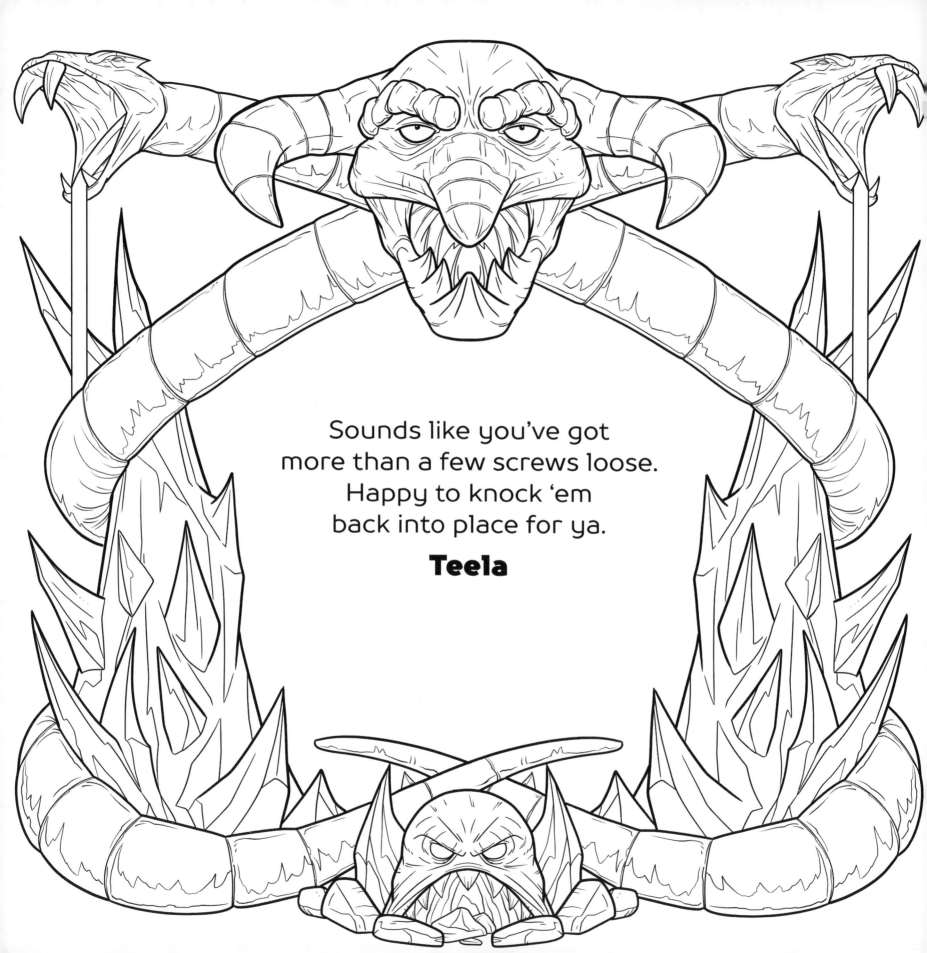

Sounds like you've got
more than a few screws loose.
Happy to knock 'em
back into place for ya.

Teela

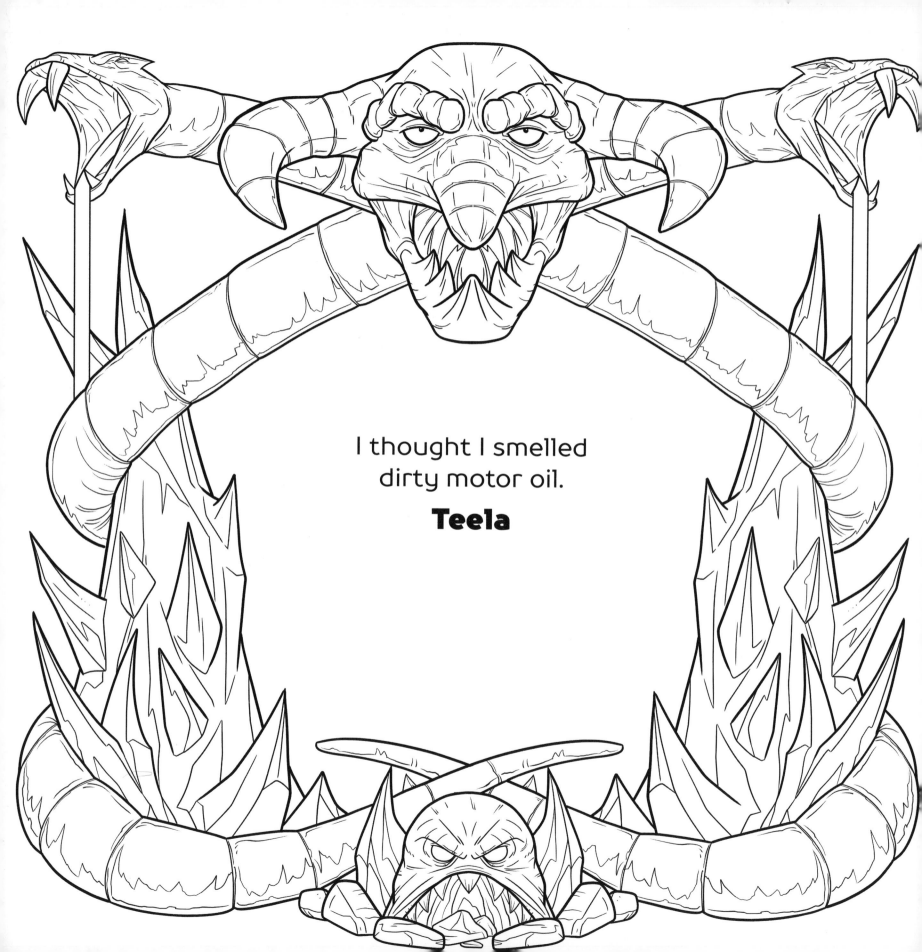

I thought I smelled
dirty motor oil.

Teela

Smell ya later!

Stinkor

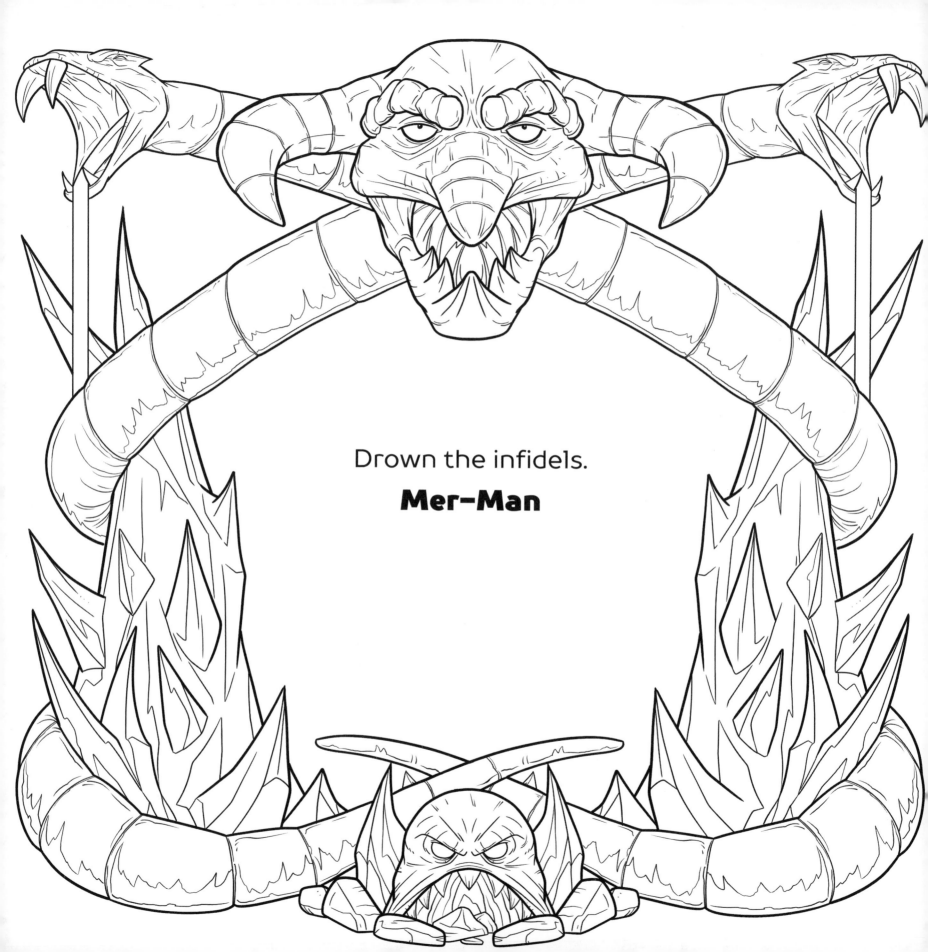

Drown the infidels.

Mer-Man

You have to fight for everything they won't give you. Your enemies, yes, but especially your friends.

Evil-Lyn

THE HISTORY OF
MASTERS OF THE UNIVERSE™

As the popularity of magic tales and epic sorcery rose in the early 1980s, Mattel created a sword-and-sorcery-themed toy line called *Masters of the Universe*™. At five and a half inches tall, He-Man and his evil nemesis Skeletor quickly became some of the world's most popular action figures. The accompanying mini-comics gave fans their first glimpse into Eternia, setting the stage for the 40-year campaign to defeat Skeletor by the Power of Grayskull.

Kids everywhere brought He-Man backpacks to school, slept on *Masters of the Universe*™ sheets, and played with their own Castle Grayskull playsets, embuing their childhoods with the epic fight of good versus evil. The television show *He-Man and the Masters of the Universe*™ was perhaps the franchise's most famous incarnation. It launched in 1983 and was followed by *She-Ra: Princess of Power*™ in 1985, which introduced fans to Prince Adam's long-lost twin sister, Adora, as she journeyed to fulfill her destiny as protector of Etheria. The franchise expanded out of animation and into the live-action movie realm with the *Masters of the Universe*™ film in 1987.

As the original fans of *Masters of the Universe*™ grew up, Eternia and Etheria stayed with them. It was Adora's story, filled with love, loss, and friendship, that was given new life in 2018 with *She-Ra and the Princesses of Power*™. The award-winning television series captured the hearts of a whole new generation.

He-Man and Skeletor continue their battle in the 2021 series *Masters of the Universe: Revelation*™, which embraces the classic 1980s mythology. This coloring book joins fans of all ages in celebrating the 40th anniversary of *Masters of the Universe*™.

The staying power of these beloved stories proves that it's not just He-Man who has the power, but it's also you, the fans, who truly have the Power of Grayskull!